A MUSIC Dream Comes True

Dear Reader

I met Straalen McCallum on Australia Day 2011, just hours before he was due to perform at a concert. He sang three songs from his first album followed by Australia's national anthem. The temperature was 43 °C but he performed with grace and professionalism. After the show, I asked him what he needed and he replied with a smile:

> "SOME WATER AND CHOCOLATE!"

That day, Straalen showed me his special presentation that he wrote to inspire other children to achieve their dreams. Follow "Straalen's Keys to Success" on pages 30–31 and I'm sure you will find inspiration to achieve your dreams, too.

I hope you enjoy reading about Straalen McCallum as much as I enjoyed writing about his exciting start in the music business.

Sharon Parsons

My sincere thanks to the following people for their time, information, images and enthusiasm for this book:

Straalen McCallum and his family, Gold Coast, Australia

Steve and Kerry White, Sydney, Australia

The team at Sony Music Entertainment Australia, Sydney, Australia

Venetta Fields, Gold Coast, Australia

Yvonne Koolis, Universal Music Publishing Pty Ltd, Sydney, Australia

Contents

A MUSIC DREAM Comes True

Straalen Sings in Sydney

It's Australia Day, 2011, in Sydney, Australia, and thousands of people line the shore of a large lake at sunset. The crowd faces the stage from many vantage points and people wonder who the next act will be. The announcer's voice silences the crowd when she says, "Please welcome to the stage the youngest singer ever to be signed by Sony Music in Australia – Straalen McCallum!"

The spotlights beam onto the 13-year-old performer who signed his first ever music recording contract six months ago. Since then, his life has been on fast forward, with song recordings and singing performances all around Australia.

STRAALEN IN DUTCH

Straalen is Dutch for "sunbeams".

AUSTRALIA

Sydney

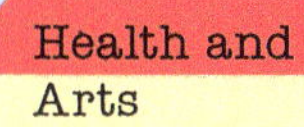

What Happens When a Boy's Voice Breaks?

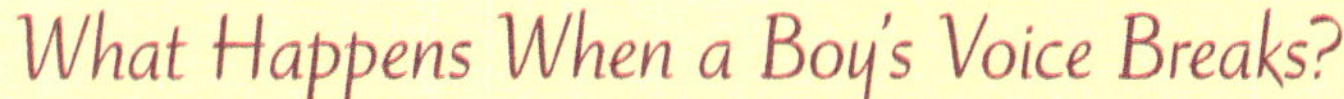

From about the age of 13, a boy's voice can "break" or change. This can happen over a period of weeks or months from soprano (a high voice) through alto to tenor (highest men's voice), baritone or even bass. Boys can continue singing during this time.

Q: SO HOW DOES A YOUNG SINGER GET THE ATTENTION OF A HUGE MUSIC COMPANY?

A: In Straalen McCallum's case, he performed for nine years in as many places as possible until one day a music producer heard his voice and said, "Hey, this boy can really sing!"

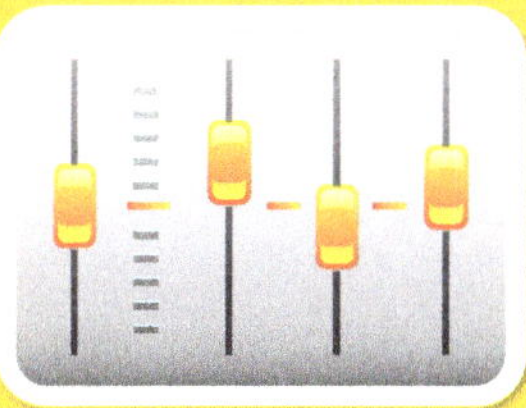

2 Straalen Surfs, Skateboards and Plays Sports

Straalen and his family live on the Gold Coast in Queensland, Australia. The family consists of Straalen's parents, two brothers and many pets, including a dog called Mantooth. When the waves are ideal for surfing, Straalen and his brothers grab their surfboards and walk down to the nearby beach.

Straalen enjoys family holidays!

Straalen on his skateboard, with Mantooth

Straalen Loves Sports

Although Straalen enjoys and excels at many sports, he also knows that it's important for vocalists to keep fit and healthy. At primary school, Straalen was the captain of the rugby team, and in his last season he scored 58 tries. I asked, "Since you have become more famous, how are you treated on the rugby field?" Straalen answers, "Well, nothing much has changed except I probably get tackled a bit harder, just for fun!"

Straalen surfs at his local beach on the Gold Coast.

Straalen even does media interviews at the beach!

3 Straalen's Dream

My dream is to sing for large audiences around the country and the world.

Straalen McCallum started singing at the age of three. He sang along to his parents' records because he loved the music. He learnt the songs off by heart – the lyrics, the melodies and the music. At kindergarten, his teachers asked him to sing all the songs he had learnt because they loved them, too. As Straalen says, "The teachers loved my songs but the kids didn't know what the heck I was singing as they weren't exactly the Wiggles's songs!"

A three-year-old Straalen performs at his first gig!

Start Dreaming

By the time Straalen was six, he knew he wanted to be a professional singer. His dream was to sing for large audiences around the country and the world. He knew that it would be very hard to achieve that dream, so to keep focused he decided to do two main things.

First, Straalen made a vision board for his bedroom wall. He chose pictures and words to inspire him, and keep him focussed on his dream.

Practise, Practise, Practise

The second thing he did was to practise a lot. Straalen practised singing every day around the house. This was easy for him because he loves music and feels a connection with the songs he chooses to sing.

Straalen's bedroom became his singing studio. He still sings every morning from 5.30 am to 6.30 am and after school, too.

Straalen loves singing along with string instruments.

Straalen's Neighbours

One of Straalen's neighbours is an elderly lady who hears him practising every morning at 5.30 am, so when he skateboards past her house, she calls out things like, "Hey Straalen, I liked your new song!"

> "YOU CAN'T GET THERE UNLESS YOU PUT IN THE HARD WORK."
>
> STRAALEN MCCALLUM

Singing in School Performances

At school, Straalen was treated just like any other kid except when it came to school concerts. Word spread quickly that Straalen had a powerful and melodic voice. He says, "I was never treated any differently at all, except that I got all the singing roles. I was never a tree in the school play, unless it sang!"

Straalen sings at a pre-school gig in the role of Hercules in Hercules the Musical.

4 Vocals with Venetta

Venetta Fields is a successful singer who lives on the Gold Coast, near Straalen's home. Since Straalen was nine years old, Venetta has been his vocal coach. So why did Venetta agree to teach this particular boy when she only worked with adults? Well, like everyone else who hears Straalen's unique voice, Venetta was captivated and said, "I'll teach him."

Vocal Coaching

Twice a week, Straalen works with Venetta on vocal techniques, learning new songs and keeping his voice strong. Straalen says, "Venetta is strict but that's good because I want to hit every note perfectly. It's a lot of hard work but it's fun!"

"Venetta is like my second mother. She has taught me so much – not only about singing, but also about the business, and life," Straalen says.

Venetta with Straalen

Straalen works on vocal techniques with Venetta

Straalen Looks After His Voice

Straalen is no different to any other vocalist – he has to look after his voice. Before a performance, Straalen warms up his voice for about ten minutes and, to protect his vocal chords, he avoids certain things – some of them are described below.

No yelling

No drinking very cold water

Straalen is ready to perform.

Avoid air-conditioned places

Avoid drinking milk

Dad Travels with Straalen

5 Straalen Gets His First Break

In 2008, when Straalen was only nine years old, he got his first break while sweeping the floor in his mother's hair salon. Straalen's mother asked him to sing for her clients, and one of them was the founder of a charity called Zig Zag. When she heard Straalen's voice, she asked him to sing at their 2008 Gala Ball. But it was at the 2009 Gala Ball when something extra-special happened.

Straalen with his family (Dad was taking the photo!)

Zig Zag Ball

At Zig Zag's 2009 Gala Ball, Straalen met the chairman of the Queensland Racing Club. The chairman was so impressed with Straalen's voice and performance that he asked him to sing at the Brisbane Cup every year. It is a major horse racing day that thousands of people attend.

Social Studies

Zig Zag

Zig Zag is a foundation based in Queensland. It donates money to charities devoted to assisting children up to 18 years of age who are sick, under privileged or at risk. It is run by volunteers, so every cent raised is passed on to children in need.

Straalen sings at a Zig Zag Gala Ball

Olivia Newton-John thanks Straalen for his performance.

Charity Concert

Another influential person happened to be at the 2009 Brisbane Cup, and he asked Straalen to sing at various events, such as at singer Olivia Newton-John's charity concert to raise money for her cancer hospital.

Straalen sings his heart out for 50 000 people before the 2010 State of Origin match.

Fifty Thousand People

At the June 2010 Brisbane Cup, in Queensland, Australia, Straalen sang the national anthem again. It was here that Straalen received another invitation to sing at one of the three State of Origin matches in front of over 50 000 people!

But unknown to Straalen, while he was singing Australia's national anthem at the State of Origin event, his biggest break was unfolding behind the scenes.

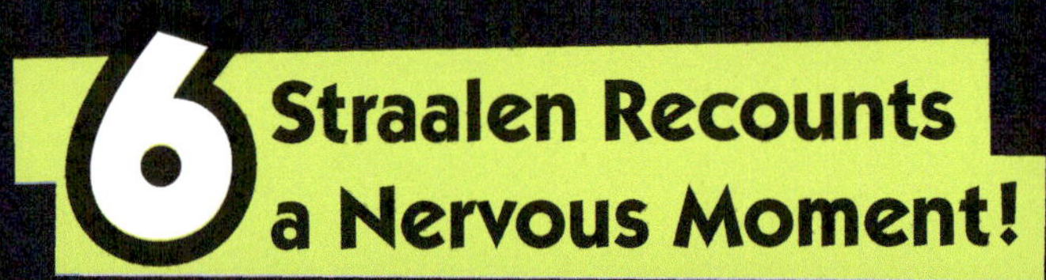

6 Straalen Recounts a Nervous Moment!

As a young singer starting out in the entertainment business, I knew that performing in front of a large audience could be quite scary. But because I also knew that it was important for my development as a professional singer, I usually felt comfortable with getting out on stage and singing my heart out.

Before 16 June 2010, the biggest audience that I had sung for was about 25 000 people. But on that day in June, I sang for over 50 000 fans at a State of Origin match in Brisbane. I got the gig when the rugby league organisers sent me an email asking if I was free to sing the national anthem. I shot back a reply saying that I sure was, and that I'd be there straight away! It was an amazing experience, but just before I was about to go on stage, things didn't quite go to plan.

You see, I'd never suffered from nerves because I'd always prepared thoroughly before every event. I'd prepared this time too, but from backstage, I took a peek at the State of Origin crowd and suddenly I felt nerves racing through my body. At first, I didn't say anything to my dad. But when I heard the producer call out to me to be ready to go on stage in twenty seconds, I felt my nerves starting to get the better of me. I whispered to Dad that I was getting nervous. He said that I'd be okay.

Then I heard the producer call out again, this time with ten seconds to go. It was so packed out there, and I was starting to feel sick. Dad gave me an "it's-going-to-be-okay" hug. My nerves were intensifying, especially when the producer called out one last time to let me know I'd be on in five seconds!

I turned to my dad again, trying not to let my panic take over. He could see how nervous I was, but said that if I was ever going to stuff up a song, now would not be the night. I cracked up laughing and went out on stage, and sung Australia's national anthem. I really enjoyed myself!

When I rejoined Dad backstage, he had the biggest smile on his face and said that I'd nailed it! I guess all I can say now is that I'm glad I didn't know that the head of Sony Music was in the crowd!

Rugby League Heroes

Ever since Straalen was a little boy, he has watched the State of Origin matches on television. But he never dreamed that he would ever perform there, or meet some of his rugby league heroes!

Straalen with Wally Lewis, a famous rugby leaguer player

Straalen having a photo taken with the Wally Lewis statue

Straalen with a famous rugby league Brisbane Broncos player, Wendell Sailor

State of Origin

Every year since 1980, two rugby league teams representing Queensland and New South Wales have competed in three games. Thousands of people attend these major sporting events in Australia and millions watch the games on television.

Straalen performing before the 2010 State of Origin match

Straalen after a long day!

After the Gig

After Straalen's biggest gig at the 2010 State of Origin match, he fell asleep in the car from Brisbane to his home on the Gold Coast.

AUSTRALIA

Brisbane

Gold Coast

7 Straalen's Biggest Break

Denis Handlin of Sony Music Entertainment Australia was very impressed by Straalen's performance at the June 2010 State of Origin. He knew he was listening to a very special voice. Denis spoke to manager Steve White, who contacted producer Garth Porter, and together they decided to contact Straalen and his parents. They invited them to the Sony Music head office in Sydney.

DENIS HANDLIN

Denis Handlin (AM), has many roles. He is Chairman and CEO of Sony Music Entertainment Australia and New Zealand, and President of Sony Music Entertainment South-East Asia and Korea.

History

Garth Porter

Garth Porter (1948–) was born in New Zealand, and played the keyboards in a popular pop band called Sherbet in the 1970s. He also helped to launch the career of Lee Kernaghan when he produced and wrote songs for him.

After signing the contract at Sony Music Entertainment Australia, Garth Porter (left) introduced Straalen to Australian country music legend, Lee Kernaghan.

Straalen's Showcase

The following week, Straalen showcased his talent for the team, including Denis Handlin, at Sony Music. It involved singing three songs and answering many questions. The team at Sony immediately knew that Straalen had an impressive vocal ability and the right attitude to succeed in the music business. So by the end of June 2010, Straalen became the youngest person to sign a recording contract with Sony. His dream had begun.

Straalen

What's your dream?

Denis Handlin with Straalen

I want to be a world-class entertainer.

Straalen sings for Sony Music's managers

History

Sony Music Australia

Since 1991, under the leadership of Denis Handlin, Sony Music Entertainment Australia has become Australia's biggest and most successful record company. In the 1990s, Sony Music stopped manufacturing vinyl records and began producing cassettes, and later CDs and DVDs.

8 Straalen Works with the Best

Studio **Recording**

Straalen spent three months with Sony, selecting songs and recording his first album. The best part of the process was being able to record songs that he has enjoyed singing for many years, as well as recording some new ones, too.

Music Producer

Garth Porter is Straalen's music producer, and they worked together to choose and record the songs for Straalen's first album. Garth's technical job in the studio is to ensure that the lyrics and the music sound just right!

> "I HAVE NEVER WORKED WITH ANYONE SO YOUNG AND SO SWITCHED ON."
>
> GARTH PORTER

Straalen takes a break.

Straalen learns how to mix the songs.

Grassroots Marketing with Gill

Gill Robert is a director at Sony Music who decides on the best marketing activities to promote Straalen to people around Australia. He says that a "grassroots marketing" campaign was required after Straalen finished the album because he was unknown to most people.

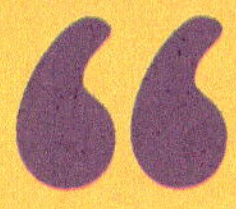

MAKING THE BEST POSSIBLE ALBUM IS JUST THE BEGINNING.

GILL ROBERT

A grassroots marketing campaign involves covering all bases, such as radio, television, press and a strong presence in music stores. A number of Sony's young artists are already known to millions of people because they have appeared in the media and on TV shows, such as *Australian Idol*.

Q: Why does Gill like working with Straalen?

A: With a smile, Gill replies, "Well, there are many reasons but here are some of them."

Straalen's just a nice, easygoing kid, and that makes it enjoyable to work with him!

He's a quick learner, because he learnt the microphone and recording techniques quickly in the studio.

He's a good listener, because you can tell Straalen something once and it sticks.

Straalen has a steely determination, and he will work hard until he sings all the notes in each song perfectly.

Music Manager

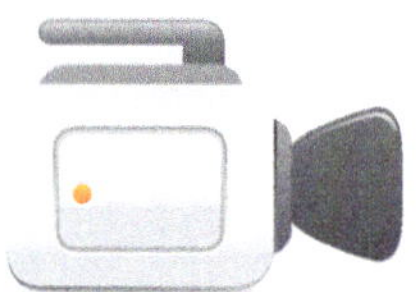

Steve White manages all of Straalen's performances around Australia – on television, at concerts, on radio, and in the print media, too.

Straalen with manager Steve White

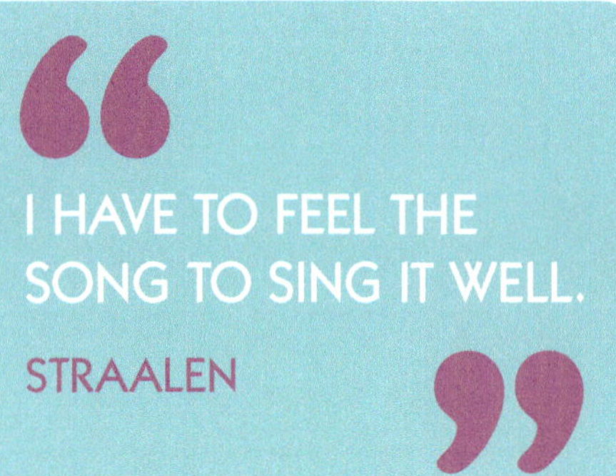

Photo Shoots

Sony Music arranges for Straalen to have promotional photographs taken for publicity purposes and for CD covers.

The make-up artist helps to get Straalen ready for a photo shoot.

Straalen at his first photo shoot

Straalen at the photo shoot for his first album

9 Magic Moments for Straalen

Straalen's manager has arranged for him to sing at many concerts and events. Many of these are to raise money for charities. Straalen has met some of his music (and tennis) idols along the way.

Straalen meets a US rock legend, Mick Fleetwood.

Straalen sings the Australian national anthem at the opening ceremony of the 2011 Australian Tennis Open.

10 Straalen's First Album

Singing "Wiyathul"

One favourite song on Straalen's first CD is called "Wiyathul". It was written by Geoffrey Gurrumul Yunupingu, who is a multi-award-winning Indigenous musician based in the Northern Territory, Australia. He granted Straalen permission to record his song on the album. After Straalen recorded the song, he sent a demo CD to Gurrumul (his traditional name) for his approval. Gurrumul was so impressed that he also asked if Straalen wanted to record a duet with him on his next album!

Geoffrey Gurrumul Yunupingu

Social Studies and Arts

Gurrumul

Geoffrey Gurrumul Yunupingu, also known as Gudjuk, was born in 1970 and has been blind from birth. A highly talented artist, he composes songs, sings and plays many musical instruments, including the drums, guitar, keyboard and the didgeridoo.

"Smile" with Straalen

One of Straalen's favourite songs is "Smile", because it has a very positive message. He has sung the song on his first album and on many occasions, such as on the Australian television show *Hey Hey It's Saturday.*

Charlie Chaplin

Charlie Chaplin's "Smile"

The music for "Smile" was composed by a famous Hollywood actor, Charlie Chaplin, for one of his movies in 1936. In 1954, John Turner and Geoffrey Parsons wrote the lyrics for the music. Since the lyrics have been available, many famous artists, such as Nat King Cole and Michael Jackson, have recorded "Smile".

Arts

"Smile" for a Movie

Charlie Chaplin (1889–1977) was born in London, UK. He wrote "Smile" as an instrumental theme for the soundtrack of his movie called Modern Times.

In 1992, a biographical movie called Chaplin was produced about Charlie Chaplin's life. The actor Robert Downey Jnr was cast to play the lead role of Charlie Chaplin. The movie traces Chaplin's childhood of extreme poverty to his rise to fame and fortune in Hollywood, USA.

“Smile” Is **Pure** Poetry

These are the original lyrics for the first verse of “Smile”. In recent years, some recording artists have adapted some of the words in the song. Normally, permission from the songwriter or publisher, and a payment is required to reproduce or change a song’s lyrics.

 Smile though your heart is **aching** 

 Smile even though it’s **breaking** 

 When there are clouds in the **sky**, 

 You’ll get **by** 

 If you smile through (with) your fear and **sorrow** 

 Smile and maybe **tomorrow** 

 You’ll see the sun come shining **through** for **you**

STRAALEN McCALLUM

A LITTLE FAITH

Straalen's first album was called A Little Faith. *His mother came up with the title for the CD because all the songs aim to inspire everyone to have a little faith in themselves to achieve their dreams.*

11 Straalen's Keys to Success

Follow **Straalen's** Pathway to Achieving **Dreams**

1. Dreams

Everyone needs to have a dream or goal. "My dream or ultimate goal is to be a really great singer and sing really great songs."

An Indigenous Dream

One of Straalen's dreams is to find a way to help more students learn about indigenous people in Australia. "They could teach us so much about our land, history, and ourselves," he says.

Straalen shows his sketch of the key points required to achieve dreams.

2. Actions

It is not enough to have a dream, we must plan a series of actions to achieve our dream. I work hard everyday to improve my vocals and singing.

Arts and Technology

Straalen's Actions

For many years, Straalen put videos of himself singing on YouTube to show his relatives in Switzerland. He said that it was a fun way of communicating with his family who lived so far away. Straalen soon noticed that other people were posting videos of his performances on YouTube, too. Word was out that he had a unique voice!

YOUTUBE

The YouTube website was created in 2005 by three friends – Steve Chen, Chad Hurley and Jawed Karim. In 2006, Google bought the YouTube company for over one billion dollars.

3. Courage

Often we need courage to do the actions required to achieve our goals or dreams. For example, I had to have the courage to stop playing some of my favourite sports and miss out on attending social events with my friends.

Straalen Doesn't Quit

When I feel like quitting because of all the hard work, I look at my vision board. It reminds me what my ultimate dreams are and gives me the courage to keep going!

4. Persistence

We all need persistence to keep doing all the actions necessary to reach our dreams. When I feel a little discouraged and nothing seems to be going right, I just keep going no matter what!

5. Consistent

When we work on being consistent with our actions it can help to achieve our goals. I had to be consistent with my singing practice every day.

6. Grace and Thankfulness

Many people don't get the opportunity to pursue their dreams. I feel very lucky and thankful for the opportunity to work on my singing career with a great team helping me along the way – my family, my vocal coach, my manager, my music company and my producer.

7. Start Achieving Dreams

> "SUCCESS COMES TO THOSE WHO BECOME SUCCESS-CONSCIOUS.
>
> STRAALEN"

Index

Glossary

chief executive officer (CEO) The leader of a company, who makes major decisions about how the company is run

marketing campaign Activities done by a company's employees to let the public know about a person or product, to try to make sales

music producer The person in a record company who selects the songs and supervises the recording of a singer's album

publicity The process of attracting the public's attention to a person or product to get their interest and support. Publicity might include interviews, articles or photo shoots.

record company A company that makes and sells music recordings

recording studio A room where music is played and recorded for an album

State of Origin A series of three rugby league matches played in Australia between the states of Queensland and New South Wales

vocal Relating to the voice and how it is used, either spoken or sung